A READING RAINBOW BOOK

DATE DUE

SAILING WITH THE WIND

SAILING WITH THE WIND

Thomas Locker

DIAL BOOKS

New York

Published by Dial Books
2 Park Avenue
New York, New York 10016

Published simultaneously in Canada by
Fitzhenry & Whiteside Limited, Toronto
Copyright © 1986 by Thomas Locker
All rights reserved.
Designed by Jane Byers Bierhorst
Printed in U.S.A.
First Edition
W
2 4 6 8 10 9 7 5 3 1

Library of Congress Cataloging-in-Publication Data

Locker, Thomas, 1937– Sailing with the wind.

Summary / A young girl discovers the ocean's majestic
character when she joins her uncle on a sailing trip.
[1. Sailing—Fiction. 2. Ocean—Fiction. 3. Uncles—Fiction] I. Title
PZ7.L7945Sai 1986 [Fic] 85-23381
ISBN 0-8037-0311-2   ISBN 0-8037-0312-0 (lib. bdg.)

The art for each picture consists of an oil painting, which is
camera-separated and reproduced in full color.

To my mother

My Uncle Jack was lucky. He worked on a big ship and traveled all over the world. Every few years when his ship came into port Uncle Jack would visit us. We had just got word that he was arriving today. I could hardly wait! I climbed a high hill so that I would be able to see his sailboat coming up the river.

I had never seen the ocean or been far away from home. But ever since I was little Uncle Jack had promised that someday we would sail down the river all the way to the ocean. Perhaps this time he would take me with him.

I sat on the hilltop, watching the clouds move across the sky. In their changing shapes I could see the wonders Uncle Jack had described to me—the Great Wall of China, gigantic blue birds from Africa, fish from the South Seas, palaces, and temple domes. Then I looked down again and saw the white sails of Uncle Jack's boat.

"Uncle Jack! Uncle Jack!" I called as I raced down the hill to the river.

We tied the boat up and Uncle Jack gave me a big hug. "Let me look at you, Elizabeth. You've gotten so big, I hardly recognize you." That was always what he said when he came.

It was a hot day. We sat outside on the porch opening Uncle Jack's presents and listening to stories of his travels. Finally at sunset a cool breeze came up and he turned to my parents. "Don't you think Elizabeth's old enough now to sail to the ocean with me?" he asked.

My father wasn't sure, but my mother said it was time I saw something of the world. At last they agreed that Uncle Jack and I would make the trip tomorrow.

My mother and I packed a picnic. Then before I went to bed Uncle Jack asked if I would help him get some things from the boat. The night had turned cool. Mist was rising from the river and it was hard to tell where the water ended and the air began.

On our way back to the house Uncle Jack said, "You'll need to set your alarm for six o'clock. It's a full day's sail to the ocean and back."

I was so excited that I couldn't fall asleep. What if my alarm clock didn't go off? But in the morning I woke up by myself at 5:30.

Uncle Jack rowed the boat out into the river just as it was starting to get light. I put on my life jacket and he raised the sails. The dawn was foggy and so quiet that I felt as if we were inside a cloud. Though there was no wind, the river's current carried us on our way.

As the sun rose, the fog disappeared and the sails filled with wind. Our boat picked up speed, moving swiftly down the river. Uncle Jack let me have a turn at the rudder and he didn't even say anything when I took off my life jacket. I had never seen this part of the river before. It was the farthest I had ever been from home.

It was almost noon and we hadn't eaten breakfast. Uncle Jack said we should have our picnic on a little island up ahead because soon we would be in the bay, away from any land. We ate sandwiches and I poured Uncle Jack some coffee. But I was in a hurry to get started again. I had seen sea gulls flying above the river and all I could think of was the ocean, waiting for me close by.

We sailed into the bay and then slowly out upon the vast blue ocean. It was more beautiful than I'd ever imagined, but our boat seemed frail and tiny as it bobbed about in the waves. The wind changed constantly and was so strong that I put my life jacket back on. "It looks like a storm is brewing," said Uncle Jack. "I think we should turn back."

The waves got higher. We went up and crashed down over and over again. The spray drenched me and I was so frightened, I felt almost sick. The wind pulled us close to the rocks, but Uncle Jack steered us safely past them back into the river. My uncle was a fine sailor. Now I felt safe again.

We sailed up the river with the wind behind us. The sky grew darker and darker and it began to rain. The storm on the ocean had been blown back to land. I had to bail the rainwater out of the boat and I got drenched all over again. There was nothing else to do but laugh. And that's exactly what Uncle Jack and I did. We had a wonderful time, laughing while the water came down in sheets.

Finally the rain stopped. The air was fresh and cool as we glided silently into our cove. The colors of the sunset shone upon the water. Never had it seemed more beautiful. I was glad to be home.

Uncle Jack stayed for about a week. He helped my father with some heavy work and spent a lot of time with me. One day we went fishing in the stream behind our house. It was high from the rain and so stirred up that we didn't catch anything. Uncle Jack began to sleep late in the morning and Mom got annoyed with him. I think Uncle Jack was just getting restless.

One morning at breakfast he announced that it was time for him to be getting back to his ship. He said good-bye to my parents and asked if I would walk him down the river.

There was so much I wanted to tell him, but I felt shy. Uncle Jack seemed to understand. "Good-bye, Elizabeth," he said. "I'll be back in a couple of years and we'll go on another adventure then. I promise."

I climbed back up the hill and watched Uncle Jack's boat until it became a tiny speck on the horizon. Then I went back to my house. I knew my parents were waiting for me and the day was just beginning.